HERACLES
THE
HERO

retold by Antonia Barber

illustrated by Peter Doherty

HERACLES THE HERO

THE LABOURS OF HERACLES

In the legends of Ancient Greece, Heracles was the son of Zeus, king of the gods, who lived on Mount Olympus. But Hera, Zeus' wife and queen of the gods, was not his mother. Zeus had fallen in love with a woman named Alcmene and tricked her by pretending he was her husband. She was expecting his baby.

One day Hera heard her husband boasting. He said that the child about to be born was his own son. He would be named Heracles and one day he would be King of Mycenae.

Hera wanted to punish Zeus for being unfaithful to her. She knew that another baby, a cousin to Heracles, would soon be born. She ensured that he was born first so that he would be king instead of Heracles.

The other baby's name was Eurystheus. He was a weak and sickly child, because he had been born prematurely; Heracles, the son of Zeus, was a healthy baby and very strong.

One night Hera tried to kill Heracles. She put two poisonous snakes in his cot, but the next morning the baby was alive and well. He was playing with the dead snakes after strangling them with his tiny hands.

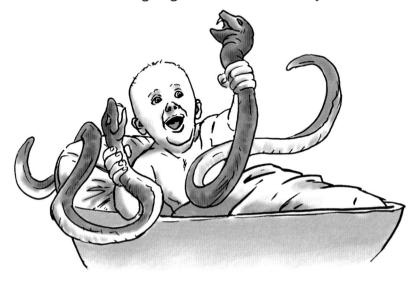

Heracles grew up to be a great hero and did many noble deeds. In time he married Megara, daughter of the King of Thebes, and had children of his own. Queen Hera saw that Zeus was proud of Heracles and his family and she became very jealous of them. She tormented the hero by inducing fits of madness and violence in him. One day, during a fit, he murdered his wife and children. When he came to his senses and saw what he had done, Heracles was horrified. Weeping, he begged the gods to forgive him.

King Zeus and Queen Hera were ashamed when they saw the result of their quarrels. They agreed that their feud must end. They decided that Heracles should be given twelve very difficult tasks. His cousin, King Eurystheus, would choose these labours. If he completed all of them, he would be freed from the guilt of the murders. Then Heracles could take his rightful place among the gods on Mount Olympus.

HOW HERACLES CLEANED THE STABLES OF KING AUGEAS

Eurystheus relished being King of Mycenae, and he was glad that he ruled the kingdom in place of his cousin Heracles. However, because he had been born prematurely, Eurystheus was never very strong or healthy. He was jealous of Heracles because he was the most popular hero in all Greece.

Eurystheus was delighted to be selected to devise twelve hard labours for Heracles. He decided to set his cousin impossible tasks that he would be certain to fail. Then the people would discover that their hero was not invincible after all.

For his first task he sent Heracles to kill a
fierce mountain lion with skin so tough that no
weapons could pierce it. Heracles simply strangled
the creature with his bare hands, and returned
wearing the lion's pelt slung over his shoulders as a
cloak. The cheering of the crowds gave King Eurystheus
a severe headache.

Next the king sent his cousin to kill the dreaded
Hydra, a fearsome monster with many heads. As one
head was cut off, two more grew in its place. The king
hoped that the Hydra would kill his cousin.

But Heracles succeeded where all other
heroes had failed. Once again King Eurystheus
was forced to listen to his people cheering
for his hated cousin.

The king pondered deeply about the third task. He learned of a wonderful deer with golden antlers that ran so swiftly that no man had ever come close to it.

"That will keep him occupied for a good while," thought Eurystheus. So he sent Heracles to catch the deer and to bring it back unharmed.

Heracles was away for an entire year. He hunted the deer over high mountains and across wide plains. At last he managed to trap it in a cave. When he saw the deer close up, it was so delicate that he was afraid to tie it up. He thought it would struggle and hurt itself. How could he get it back to Mycenae?

Heracles prayed for help to Artemis, the goddess of wild creatures. Artemis was touched by the gentleness of the strong man and she told the deer to follow him without fear. Heracles led it safely back to Mycenae and a hero's welcome.

King Eurystheus was displeased to see his cousin. He sent him on a fresh errand to capture a wild boar. This creature was destroying crops in a far-off mountain kingdom. King Eurystheus was anticipating a long spell of peace and quiet.

To his annoyance, Heracles was soon back. He had trapped the wild boar in a net, tied it up securely, and carried it back to Mycenae on his shoulders.

As Heracles entered the palace, Eurystheus turned around. He saw the huge beast with its angry yellow eyes close behind him. In terror, the king leapt into a huge jar. All the people roared with laughter together with Heracles.

Slowly Eurystheus emerged from the jar, his face red with shame. His hatred of Heracles grew fiercer.

"His next labour will not allow him to be brave and heroic," thought Eurystheus. "I will devise something really disgusting!"

"Well done, cousin," he said to Heracles, "you have earned a good rest. Your next task shall be a simple one and free from all danger. You shall pay a visit to my friend King Augeas, and while you are there, you must spend one day, no more, cleaning out his stables."

Heracles frowned. He did not like the sound of this task. Killing and capturing fierce monsters was work fit for a hero, not mucking out stables! He heard a ripple of laughter. Some at court were jealous of the hero's popularity, and were amused at the thought of him shovelling horse manure and cow dung. He had no choice, though. He must serve his punishment however unpleasant it might be. As he set out, he comforted himself with the thought that the task could not be too taxing. After all, it would only last for a day.

The kingdom of Elis, where Augeas ruled, lay on the far side of the mountains. Heracles climbed over the high pass and began to make his way down into the valley. As he went he noticed a most unpleasant smell. The valley was very beautiful and fertile with two sparkling rivers running down, one on either side of the mountains. All this loveliness, however, could not compensate for the foul stench that filled the air.

When Heracles came to a village and stopped for refreshments, he enquired about the stink from the innkeeper. The man sighed.

"It comes from the stables of our King Augeas," he declared. "His beasts have been sadly neglected. The stables have not been cleaned for years. Now they lie many feet deep in dung. Even worse, it has spread onto all the land around. It has poisoned the fields and clogged up the rivers."

"Can nothing be done?" asked Heracles.

The innkeeper shook his head. "No man could clean it now," he stated, "not if he worked for a hundred years!"

Then Heracles knew that he had been deceived by his cousin. This task would be the most formidable yet, and how could it be accomplished in a single day?

He thanked the innkeeper and proceeded down the valley. With every step, the awful stench grew worse, even though his destination was still some distance away in an adjacent valley.

Inside the palace the rooms were filled with mounds of scented flowers. Augeas lay on a heap of cushions while servants sprayed perfumes in the air around him.

The king welcomed Heracles, for the fame of the hero had spread through all the length and breadth of Greece.

"To what do we owe the honour of your visit?" he enquired.

Heracles told Augeas of the task which Eurystheus had set for him. The king and his courtiers roared with laughter when he heard about the challenge.

"Clean out my stables?" said Augeas. "And in a single day? I would give a tenth of my flock to any man who could accomplish that! But a great hero should not dirty his hands with such a task!"

Heracles also felt the task was unworthy of him.

"I only ask your permission to carry out this task," he told Augeas coldly. "It is for me to decide whether or not I shall make my hands dirty."

"Then be my guest," replied the king. "You will find plenty of shovels down in the stables. Let us hope they are not buried beneath all the dung!"

He thought this was very witty and all his courtiers shrieked with laughter. His visitor strode out in disgust.

Heracles made his way down to the stables. The dung spread deep and wide and the stench was almost more than he could bear. All the animals were covered in filth. Heracles lost no time. He gathered the flocks and herds together. Those creatures trapped in the slurry Heracles lifted out with his bare hands.

When they were all freed, he drove the animals up the mountainside and washed them clean in the river. He watched with pleasure as the muck that had covered the poor beasts was swept away down the hillside.

Then as he watched, an ingenious plan came to him. He had thought of a way to clean out the stables in a single day. Better still, it could be done without soiling his hands!

Leaving the clean animals to roam free, Heracles made his way down to a point just above the stable yard. Here he began to pick up huge rocks that no other man could have lifted. Carrying them upon his back he started to build a wall. He worked for many hours without respite. As the wall grew, it made a dam, trapping the waters of the two rivers. The dam rose higher and higher.

When the wall reached above his head, Heracles was satisfied. He left it and began another task. Still using only his bare hands, he tore huge rocks out of the ground. He made a deep gully running from the foot of the dam to the back of the stable. Then he made a very large gap in the stable wall.

When he had completed all this labour, he returned to the dam and rested. He smiled as he watched the lake growing wider and deeper.

Late in the afternoon, the water from the two rivers reached the top of the wall and began to spill over. Then Heracles tore a tall tree out of the ground and stripped off all the branches. He walked along the top of the wall he had made. He used the tree trunk to knock out the rocks in the centre of the wall. With a thundering roar the water poured out and flowed in a great rush into the gully that Heracles had made. It surged down the hillside towards the stables, forcing its way in through the gap in the back wall. It swept through the stables carrying all the muck before it.

Some of the water swirled around the sides of the building. It flooded the fields washing away the poisonous, stinking slurry. The torrent flowed for hours.

Heracles moved through the flood carrying huge boulders. He blocked the flow in one place and released it in another. He sent the waters this way and that until every last corner was clean.

Then Heracles took down the great wall of the dam. He lifted the huge rocks and used them to fill in the gully. He sent the two rivers flowing back into their old channels. The stables stood clean and bright in the sunlight. The land was fresh and sweet smelling. The rivers ran clear and sparkling. All the muck and filth was swept far away down the valley. When it reached the distant sea, it sank without trace beneath the blue waves.

When Augeas saw what Heracles had done he was astonished. However, he did not honour his promise and give him the tenth of his flocks.

"Had I not let you clean my stables you could not have completed your 'task'," he said. "Therefore, I owe you nothing."

Heracles made his way home to Mycenae. When he reported the story of how he'd cleaned the stables, no one mocked him. They were amazed by his cunning and his strength. "We might have had a king who was clever as well as brave and strong," they murmured.

King Eurystheus overheard what his people said and his hatred of Heracles grew ever stronger.

THE GOLDEN APPLES OF HESPERIDES

King Eurystheus of Mycenae was deeply discontented. He was jealous of his cousin Heracles, who was a great hero.

Zeus, king of the gods, had ordered Heracles to undertake twelve difficult labours, and Eurystheus was to choose them. He had set his cousin dangerous tasks which he thought would be impossible. He had sent Heracles to fight dangerous monsters hoping that they might kill him, but Heracles had succeeded every time.

Eurystheus was becoming desperate.

There were but two further tasks to be achieved. If Heracles succeeded, he would join the gods on Mount Olympus. Eurystheus could not bear to think of his cousin attaining such a great honour. How could he turn the gods against Heracles?

"The goddess Hera once loathed Heracles," he thought, "but she has promised her husband Zeus that she will not persecute him further. If Heracles offends her again, perhaps she might have second thoughts."

Then, the king recalled Hera's favourite gift – a tree bearing golden apples which Gaia, the Mother of Earth, had created for her. It was guarded by a deadly serpent with a hundred heads, yet no one knew where the tree was located.

"I'll send Heracles to secure the golden apples," thought the king. "With any luck, he will never even find them. If he does, the serpent will almost certainly kill him. If by some chance he does steal Hera's apples, she will be furious, and she will never allow him take his place among the gods."

When Heracles learned of his task, he set out without knowing which road to take. Crossing a river, he met some water nymphs and asked them for assistance. They suggested he seek out Nereus, the Old Man of the Sea. He was one of the old gods, called the Titans, who had created the earth long before the gods of Olympus were born. The old gods and the new gods had fought and the old gods had been defeated, but they were wise and had always been friendly towards men.

"Nereus lives in the depths of the ocean," the nymphs told Heracles, "but occasionally he rests in the sun on a sandy beach. If you find him, you must seize him before he can vanish beneath the waves. But beware! For he can change his shape in a moment and he will do all he can to escape you."

Heracles thanked the nymphs and made his way down to the sea-shore. There he found the Old Man of the Sea, peacefully dozing in the sun. Silently Heracles crept closer until he could grab him. As he put his arms around Nereus, he found that he was embracing a huge fish. As he tightened his grip it became a slippery eel. When he seized the eel, he found that he was holding a tentacle of a huge octopus. For a long time the struggle continued, but Heracles would not let go.

At last the old god grew tired and changed back into his own shape.

"You are a very determined man," Nereus said admiringly. "What gives you the strength to hold me so long against my will?"

Then Heracles told of his quest to find the golden apple tree and the reason Zeus and Hera had given him the twelve labours to perform.

Nereus sighed. "These new gods are proud and demanding," he said. "Before they came we lived at peace with mankind. You are a brave man and I will assist you."

The old god told Heracles that the tree grew in the garden of the Hesperides. The Hesperides were beautiful maidens who dwelled in the land of the sunset. Nereus informed Heracles of the road he must travel and as they parted, the old god warned him of the dangers that might lie ahead.

For many weeks Heracles walked westward until he reached a range of high mountains. Slowly he climbed to the top and there he came upon another of the Titans. He was chained to a rock, groaning horribly as a huge eagle pecked at his liver. Heracles recognised him immediately. This was Prometheus who had always been a true friend of mankind. Zeus had refused to give men the gift of fire; instead he left them to freeze in winter and to feed on raw flesh. But Prometheus, who hated the new gods, had taken pity on mankind. He had stolen fire from the gods and given it to man. It was for this that Zeus had condemned him to suffer forever.

With no thought for the anger of Zeus, Heracles took his bow and sent an arrow flying straight into the eagle's heart. When it lay lifeless on the ground, Heracles broke the chains and set Prometheus free.

"You are surely a fearless hero," said the Titan. "Few men would risk the wrath of Zeus as you have done for me!"

The hero smiled. "I am Heracles," he said, "and I honour the debt all men owe you. We would still be living like animals without your gift of fire."

Prometheus laughed. "Then let us put it to good use," he said.

He lit a fire and they roasted the great eagle over it. As they sat together in the firelight tearing the rich meat from the bones, Heracles told Prometheus of his quest for the golden apples and how Nereus had guided him on his way.

To his dismay, the Titan shook his head.

"No man can steal the golden apples," he said.

"I am not afraid of the serpent," said Heracles. "I have killed the many headed Hydra and a three headed giant with six arms, and other fearsome monsters!"

"I do not doubt your courage," said Prometheus. "But only gods and goddesses can enter the magic garden of the Hesperides."

Heracles was very downcast. "I shall never attain the status of a god unless I can secure the apples."

There was a long silence. Then Prometheus began hesitantly,

"Perhaps there is a way ..."

"Tell me!" said Heracles eagerly.

"You must seek help from another of my kin, the great Atlas. He is the Titan who bears the weight of the heavens upon his shoulders. You must request him to fetch the apples for you. He may enter the garden."

Heracles thanked him for his advice.

They ate their fill, slept, and when morning came, took leave of each other and Heracles continued on his way.

Heracles travelled many leagues until he reached the great Atlas mountains where he found the mighty Atlas standing upon the highest peak. Though he could not move, lest the heavens should fall, the Titan could talk and he was delighted to converse with a visitor. Few people ever climbed so high and his life was a lonely one.

He listened intently as Heracles told him of his adventures. When he heard how his fellow Titan had been set free, he shed tears of joy.

"Prometheus suggested that I seek your help," said Heracles. "He warned me that only gods can enter the garden of the Hesperides and said that I should request you to fetch the apples for me."

Atlas sighed and the heavens rocked. "There is nothing I should like more than to help you," he said. "But I dare not move from this mountain peak. When we Titans were defeated by the new gods, I was condemned for ever to stand here and bear the weight of the heavens upon my back. If you could free me, as you freed Prometheus, I would gladly fetch the apples for you."

"Then let me take the heavens upon my back," said Heracles. "I cannot free you forever, but I am sure I could bear the weight for a short period."

Atlas laughed and the heavens rocked even more.

"You are a mere man," he said. "Do you think you have the strength of a Titan?"

The hero frowned. "I am the strongest man in Greece," he said. "Some say I am the strongest man in all the world!"

"And what do you say?" asked the Titan.

"I say I am sufficiently strong to hold up the heavens," declared Heracles.

"Then let us try you," said Atlas, "and pray you are right! For if not, the weight of the heavens will crush you like a beetle!"

The Titan bent his back until he was the same height as Heracles. Then as he moved sideways he eased the burden from his shoulders. Heracles gasped as he felt the full weight of the heavens upon him. He gritted his teeth and began to draw himself up to his full height again.

Atlas watched, fascinated. He stretched his arms and twisted his shoulders. It felt wonderful to be free of his load for the first time in so many decades.

"How long will it take you to fetch the golden apples?" asked Heracles, trying not to sound too anxious.

"Oh, a week or so," said Atlas carelessly.

Heracles longed to beg him to hurry, but he did not like to admit that he found the weight a burden.

A week passed and with each day the load grew heavier. Perhaps Atlas would never come back again. The hero groaned under the weight. He felt that the heavens would crush him.

At the end of the second week, Atlas reappeared. Heracles was very relieved when he saw him ascending the mountainside. At last he could rid himself of the terrible weight of the heavens.

But Atlas was not at all anxious to relieve him.

"I should like to enjoy my freedom a little longer," he told Heracles, "so I have decided to take the golden apples to King Eurystheus myself."

Heracles was horrified. He needed to rid himself of the weight before it destroyed him. He thought rapidly. "I would be happy to bear the heavens for a little longer, my friend, but there is a sore patch on my left shoulder. Take back the weight for a moment while I make a small pad of cloth to cover the spot."

Atlas resumed his burden, the full weight of the heavens.

As soon as he was free, Heracles straightened his back, then bent down and picked up the golden apples.

"I would not willingly deceive you," he told Atlas, "but I must take these myself in order to complete my task. However, I give you my word that I will remember you when I become a god on Mount Olympus, and I will plead with my father Zeus to set you free."

Atlas groaned when he realised that he had been tricked, but there was nothing he could do. He knew that he must bear his own burden again.

Heracles made his way back to Mycenae and presented the golden apples to King Eurystheus.

Now the king had never imagined that Heracles would succeed in his task. When he saw the golden apples he began to tremble. What would the queen of the gods do when she found that her apples had been stolen?

"Will she blame Heracles," he wondered, "or will she blame me for dispatching him to fetch them?"

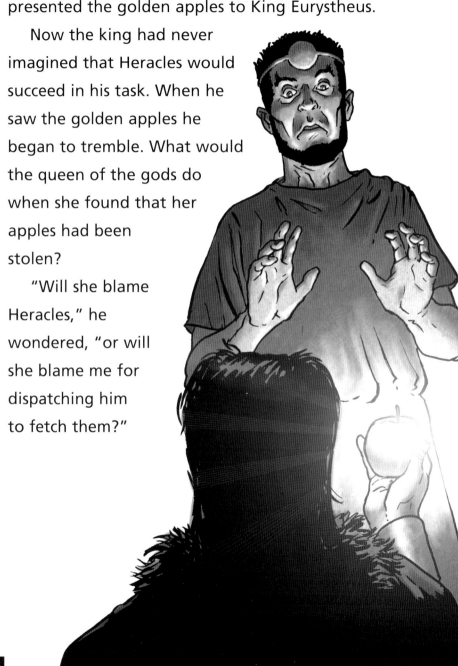

Terrified, he refused to accept the apples. He sought refuge in his bedroom and locked himself inside.

When Eurystheus had departed, Heracles stood and stared at the golden apples in his hands. He did not want to anger Hera again. He had spent most of his life tormented by the queen of the gods. For a long time he pondered. Then he bore the golden apples to the temple of the goddess Athene, who had helped him in the past. He laid them upon her altar and left them there.

Athene was much too wise to fall out with Hera! She ordered Hermes, who was the messenger of the gods, to return the golden apples to the garden of the Hesperides.

So, after the arduous labour of Heracles, the apples were safely back where they had always been. Now, only one last task remained for the hero before he earned his place among the gods.

HERACLES IN THE UNDERWORLD

King Eurystheus of Mycenae had devised eleven of the twelve hard labours for his cousin Heracles to perform. The king was jealous of his cousin and longed to see him fail so the people would mock him.

He had hoped that Heracles might be killed by one of the fearsome monsters he had been sent to slaughter or capture. However, Heracles had triumphed every time with the result that the people of Mycenae hero-worshipped him. They wished Heracles could be king in place of Eurystheus, a nervous, sickly and unimaginative leader.

Now the king was at his wit's end for he had only one last challenge to set. If Heracles were to succeed this time, Zeus, king of the gods, had assured him a place among the gods on Mount Olympus.

The king looked far and wide for a truly fearsome monster, but Heracles had already killed or tamed most of them. The few that remained would be child's play for such a proven hero!

Eurystheus shut himself away and brooded at length. Then he had an inspiration. It was so daring that he feared the gods might not allow it. He would send Heracles into the Underworld, the land of the dead!

If the world of the living held no more monsters to challenge a hero, then he would order him to bring back Cerberus. For surely no living man could overcome the huge three-headed dog that guarded the iron gates to the Kingdom of Hades; only the dead could pass into that dark Underworld.

"My cousin will never succeed this time," thought the king gleefully. "He will either return defeated or, if I am even more fortunate, Cerberus will kill him. Either way I shall be satisfied."

If Eurystheus thought that his cousin would turn ashen when he spelled out his final task, he was wrong. For a moment the hero was speechless with astonishment. Then he laughed abruptly and a strange light came into his eyes.

"At last!" he cried. "At last a task worthy of a hero! When I have done this last labour even the gods will honour me. None will deny my right to dwell among them."

The first challenge for Heracles was to locate the secret entrance to the Underworld. He sought help from the goddess Athene who had aided him previously in moments of need. The goddess told him that he must go to the Temple at Eleusis. There he must perform secret rituals in honour of the goddess Demeter. It was her daughter, Persephone, who was wife to Hades and Queen of the Underworld.

Once this had been carried out, Athene asked
Hermes, the messenger of the gods, if he would guide
Heracles. Only Hermes could pass freely between
Olympus, Earth and the Underworld.

Hermes agreed, and he and Heracles set out
together. Their road took them into distant, rugged
mountains. They passed into dark caverns beneath the
earth and down steps hewn from the rock below. At
times Heracles had to feel his way in darkness as he
followed Hermes. The god seemed to be able to discern
his way without light. Sometimes the hero saw a
strange, unearthly glow around him, red and
flickering as if fires burned in the caverns below.

At last their path brought them to the bank of a wide river. Here they found a boat rowed by Charon, the ferryman of the Underworld. It was his job to ferry dead mortals across the river Styx in return for a small silver coin. On the other side of the river loomed the great iron gates of the Underworld, and before them stood the dreaded Cerberus guarding the gates against all living men.

Hermes had warned Heracles that he must not try to steal Cerberus.

"You must seek out King Hades in his palace and ask his consent," he told the hero. "Without it, it would be impossible for you to escape from the Underworld."

First Heracles had to make his way in. He had brought with him three big pieces of meat. Hidden inside were poppy seeds. He threw a piece of meat to each of the three heads which seized them eagerly. Heracles and Hermes waited and watched until the heads began to droop and one by one their eyes closed. Then Heracles crept past the sleeping hound and pushed at the great iron gates of the Underworld. The gates creaked as they swung open and the dog twitched. Luckily, Cerberus didn't wake and was soon still again. Heracles passed through into the land of the dead: the gates clanged shut behind him. He followed Hermes through the dimly lit caverns. Thin figures of the dead moved about them. In the distance they saw two stone seats with men bound to them with ropes.

"They are the Seats of Forgetfulness," said Hermes. "The men who sit there will slowly forget everything until at last they are turned to stone."

"What have they done to deserve such a fate?" enquired Heracles.

"They tried to carry off Queen Persephone," said Hermes.

As Heracles came closer he recognised one of them. It was Theseus who had once helped him in the past. The man cried out and Heracles took pity on him. He slashed the ropes with his sword but at once the ground began to heave and crack beneath his feet.

"King Hades grows angry," warned Hermes. So Heracles passed quickly on his way.

When they reached the palace, Hermes led Heracles into the throne room. Here sat the dark king of the Underworld on a black marble throne with his lovely queen at his side. He frowned at the sight of a living man. Heracles looked strong and powerful among the pale shades of the dead who thronged the room.

"You are welcome as ever," said King Hades to Hermes, "but the living have no place in my kingdom. By what right do you bring this mortal into my presence?"

"This is the great hero Heracles," Hermes informed him. "By the will of Zeus he was given twelve labours to perform. All but one he has completed with his strength and courage. The last one brings him, through no will of his own, to brave the terrors of the Underworld. Deal with him kindly, my lord, for he has many wondrous tales to tell."

The king's face brightened at these words. Time passed wearily in the land of the dead. A good storyteller was a welcome visitor.

So Hades greeted Heracles politely and Persephone invited the hero and his guide to dine with them. The feast was very splendid but the food lacked flavour. The wine flowed like water but tasted almost as weak. It seemed that everything in the land of shadows was a poor reflection of the living world above.

When the meal was over, Heracles kept the king and queen enthralled with stories of his brave deeds. As Hades listened he grew nervous at the thought of a man of such strength and courage loose in his fragile kingdom. He resolved to send the hero back into the land of the living.

So when Heracles finished his stories and told Hades the purpose of his visit, the king heard him with interest.

"My final task is to take back Cerberus who guards the gates of your kingdom," said Heracles. "Unless I can show him alive to my cousin Eurystheus, all my other deeds will count for nought."

King Hades frowned and thought for a while. "Without Cerberus my land would be unguarded. Without him the dead might leave this realm and go wandering about the world of the living."

"I will take the dog swiftly to Mycenae," promised Heracles. "I undertake to return him the moment my task is completed."

Hades sat in silence. He stared at the powerful man with his club and his sword and his bow and arrows. The thought of him with the great three-headed dog in his power was alarming.

"Lay down your arms," he commanded. When Heracles looked as if he might refuse, the king added, "I must be certain that the dog will not be harmed."

Heracles hated to part with his weapons. Hades was a god, though, and the hero had no choice. He laid his weapons at the king's feet.

Hades smiled. He sent a servant to fetch a leash. It had three collars, each one armed with sharp spikes.

"If you can attach this to the beast and persuade him to accompany you," he said, "you may take him to Mycenae." He turned to Hermes. "And I charge you, my lord, to see that he is safely returned."

Heracles thanked the king and took the leash. With Hermes to guide him, he made his way back to the iron gates. As they went Heracles wondered how he could put the leash on Cerberus. He thought of all the other monsters he had overcome. Some he had killed with his weapons, but now he had no weapons. He had strangled a ferocious lion with his bare hands, but how could he seize a dog with three heads? While he gripped one the others would be tearing at his flesh. The king had said that he must persuade the dog to go with him. So he could not tie it up and carry it on his back as he had once carried a huge wild boar. Somehow he would have to persuade Cerberus to go to Mycenae with him.

As they came through the iron gates, the huge dog was looking the other way. He was watching a boatload of the newly dead as Charon ferried them across the river.

Heracles crept up behind and threw himself onto the dog's broad back. Swiftly he fastened one of the collars around the middle neck. Cerberus went mad! He leapt and twisted and turned trying to throw the hero off his back. But Heracles hung on with all his strength. The two other heads turned and snapped at him, showing their fearsome teeth. Heracles seized another neck and struggled to put on the second collar. Just as he fastened it, the third head sank its teeth into his shoulder.

Heracles gave a great roar of pain, but he fought on until at last all three heads wore their spiked collars. Swiftly he tied the leash to the great iron gates. Then, careful to keep out of reach, he walked round until he faced Cerberus. The great dog leaped and howled as it tried to reach him. The iron gates rattled with the force of each pull.

Heracles sat on the ground just beyond the reach of the angry jaws. He waited until Cerberus had worn himself out with barking. Then he spoke quietly to the great hound.

"I mean you no harm," he said. "Your master, King Hades, has given me permission to take you for a walk. Your fame is so great in the world of men that the people long to see you for themselves."

Cerberus was astonished and very flattered. In all the years that he had guarded the Underworld, no one had ever come to take him for a walk! He sat down quietly and looked hopefully at Heracles. The three heads panted eagerly.

"If you will promise not to bite me again," said the hero, ruefully rubbing his sore shoulder, "I will untie you and we will be on our way."

Cerberus wagged his tail and the three heads yapped excitedly.

Carefully Heracles took hold of the leash and was nearly pulled off his feet as the huge dog rushed towards the landing stage. Charon refused to take a dog in the boat so Cerberus had to swim alongside. He pulled the boat with such strength that the old ferryman did not need to row as they passed over into the land of the living.

They made their way back through the underground caverns, up the many stone steps and out into the light of day. Cerberus was enjoying his walk as much as any other dog. He wanted to sniff and explore everything.

He tugged the leash this way and that, pulling Heracles behind him. Any other man would have been dragged helplessly along the ground. But the hero's strength and his powerful arms were a match for the three-headed beast.

After a few hours Cerberus began to tire and they settled down to a fast walking pace. By now they had come down from the mountains. They began to pass through little villages and then larger towns.

The people who saw them coming were terrified at first. When, however, they saw that Heracles had the huge dog under control, they began to run behind, shouting and laughing in their astonishment.

Back at his palace, King Eurystheus waited for his cousin's return. He never doubted for a moment that Heracles would fail. How could any living man bring back Cerberus, the guardian of the Underworld?
He heard the sound of a crowd approaching. He heard the shouting and the laughter and the king was delighted.

"The people are mocking him!" he thought to himself. "He has come home defeated and they are all laughing at him. Now I shall see him humbled. Now he will never be a god!"

The king called up all his courtiers. He led them in a great crowd into the entrance hall of the palace. "We too will welcome my cousin home with our laughter!" he said.

Heracles knocked at the great doors of the palace. Eurystheus waited eagerly as the doors swung open. There, just a few feet from him, stood the huge three-headed monster, Cerberus, straining at the leash. Holding the other end was the laughing figure of his hated cousin Heracles!

The great dog was whining and slobbering with excitement, but the king thought it was about to attack him.

With a shriek of horror, Eurystheus ran through the palace until he reached the safety of his bedroom. Then all his people howled with laughter but not as the king had hoped they would. They were mocking him – their king – not Heracles. As if that were not bad enough, his cousin had now completed the last of his labours.

Eurystheus cried tears of rage as he listened to the wild celebrations which rang out all around him.

Now nothing could stand in the way of Heracles. He was the true son of Zeus and would be welcomed by all the gods on Mount Olympus.

THE TWELVE LABOURS OF HERACLES

Heracles completed all twelve tasks set for him by King Eurystheus. He showed enormous strength, courage and cunning. Once his tasks were completed, Zeus, his father and king of the gods, took Heracles to join the other gods on Mount Olympus.

1 Kill the lion of Nemea

2 Kill the many-headed Hydra

3 Capture the Ceryneian Hind

4 Kill the wild boar of Erymanthus

5 Clean the Augean Stables

Kill the carnivorous birds of Stymphalis

Capture the wild bull of Crete

Capture the man-eating mares of Diomedes

Obtain the girdle of Hippolyte

Capture the oxen of Geryon

Take the golden apples from the Garden of Hesperides

Bring Cerberus, the dog of the Underworld,
to the living world

PRONUNCIATION GUIDE

Alcmene	*say*	alk-**meen**-ee
Artemis	*say*	**are**-te-miss
Athene	*say*	a-**thee**-nee
Augeas	*say*	awe-**jee**-us
Cerberus	*say*	**sir**-ber-us
Ceryneian	*say*	**sair**-ee-nee-an
Charon	*say*	**ka**-ron
Diomedes	*say*	die-om-**ee**-deez
Eleusis	*say*	ih-**loo**-sis
Erymanthus	*say*	air-ee-**man**-thus
Eurystheus	*say*	you-**riss**-thyoos
Gaia	*say*	**guy**-a
Geryon	*say*	gair-**eye**-on
Hera	*say*	**hair**-a

Heracles	*say*	**hair**-a-kleez
Hermes	*say*	**her**-meez
Hesperides	*say*	hess-**pair**-re-dees
Hippolyte	*say*	hip-**pol**-ee-tee
Hydra	*say*	**hi**-dra
Megara	*say*	**meg**-er-a
Mycenae	*say*	my-**see**-nee
Nemea	*say*	**ne**-me-ya
Nereus	*say*	**near**-ee-us
Olympus	*say*	oh-**limp**-us
Prometheus	*say*	prom-**ee**-thee-us
Stymphalis	*say*	stim-**fal**-is
Thebes	*say*	theebz
Zeus	*say*	zyoos